Plants
vs
Zombies
The Beginning

Plants
vs
Zombies
The Beginning

Table of contents

Saturday

'Moanday. Moanday. Moanday.'

Zombie Steve was being shaken. He tried to hide under the warm cosy duvet. Whilst attempting to pull it over his head and burying his head in to the pillow at the same time.

'Moannnnn-dayyyyy'.

More shaking now. 'No!' grumped Steve.

'Moanday! You're late for school. Mums gonna be mad at you' said Eliza who now was shaking Steve with both hands.

'Quit it Zah. Quit it, I'm getting up now'.

'Don't look like it to me. Hurry up'.

'Alright!'

Eliza ran out of the room and thundered down the stairs at a ferocious speed. Steve yanked off the cover and sat on the bed scratching his head in some vague attempt to wake himself up. Hearing the murmurings of Eliza and Mum talking downstairs, Steve strolled out making his way to the bathroom.

'Hello Son. What have you got planned today?' Asked David in (what Steve thought) was a very happy manner, especially as it's a School day after all.

'School' grumped Steve.

'On a Saturday? Your keen. Wow, so will it be Dr. Steve soon?'

'Uh?' questioned Steve.

'It's Saturday.'

'Uh?' repeated Steve.

'Ben...it...is...Saturday...Today....Sat-ter-day, you know Sat-tastic day'.

'I will strangle her!' Shouted Steve. David looked puzzled, but laughter from downstairs filtered up and both David and Steve looked down to see Eliza run off towards the kitchen.

Enlightenment dawned on David's face. 'She done it again Steve. Hey? She convinced you it was Monday? Oh Steve, Oh Steve. She done it again!' laughed David. 'I'm tired' said Steve turning around to return to the warm cosy safety of his bed. But Steve wasn't moving. In fact, he was beginning to lean backwards.

The reason? A hand had grabbed his shirt.

'Since you are up Son you might as well join us for breakfast. Come on' Turning Steve around to face the bathroom 'Wash your face and hands and get the mud off of it and join us for a family breakfast'. With that statement set in stone David walked downstairs leaving the bewildered Steve to ponder revenge on his sister.

With the Draka Zombie family, or perhaps clan (as David likes to say) more awake now and having some warm-(ish) fried worms and grack juice, Saturday's plans were being discussed around the table in-between the crunching of worms, clanking of cutlery and the smell of Katie's homemade swamp grimmer tea. Steve's grumpiness slowly evaporated, due to some food and juice. The fact that it is Saturday and sunny! Finally combined with Eliza's non-stop energy.

Steve agreed to join Eliza and go over to see Chloë and hang out at the playing field. David and Katie were debating the potential raucous, fallouts and even debauchery of tonight's Annual Berry Hunter scare party which Katie told David it's just an excuse for old zombies to wear a sheet and act like animal house'.

'But this year it'll be different.' Said Steve.

'On what grounds? I'm all ears?' said Katie, with a small but noticeable tone of cynical disbelief.

'It's a different sheet?' pleaded David with a smile so cheeky and friendly that even if David were caught with his hand in the rotten jam jar, rotten jam sauce smeared over his face and wearing a T-shirt proclaiming him to be *The Original Scare Zombie King*, he would be allowed to continue. So, he did. Also, I'll make a leaf crown thingy'.

Katie looked at Eliza and Steve 'your zombie father means a Civic Crown made out of oak leaves'. Looking back at David now 'not ivy'.

Feeling rather little David replied, 'that's right Kay-dee' With a grunt sound at Katie 'I will be making my...Civic Crown...

today. And not using the Ivy that is on the table next to a wire coat hanger'.

'Well so be it. But if you come back in the state you did last year I will take that crown and....'

A knocking at the door interrupted the conversation. Perhaps interrupting at the most opportune moment, especially given the age group and civilized zombies around the table.

'Mr and Mrs Draka, Hello. Chloë here. Hello?'

Having washed and cleaned and helped tidy the breakfast and kitchen area, Eliza and Steve were now in the playing field with Chloë looking for adventures.

Around 12.00 as bellies began to make their existence known through the language of gurgling and groaning Steve casually mentioned 'last week-- I saw two zombies walking on the path behind our house'.

'What!' sparked Eliza. 'Tell me more?'

'Yeah more' contributed Chloë.

'They walked past our back gate and up the track-'
'And?' hurried Eliza.
'And, across the field to the Farm'.
Eliza's mouth dropped open. Recovering from this shock she continued, 'Across the field to the Zombie Scare Farm?'
'Yeah' Astonished that she wasn't told this critical piece of information when it originally occurred, Eliza stared at Steve. 'Let's go then!'
'Where?' asked Steve
'To the Farm you numpty' said Chloë Eliza stood up, breathed in hard (hoping that a breeze will appear right now to blow her hair in the wind, (*but sadly no*), raised her zombie arm as if throwing a flaming javelin and pointed toward the general direction of the Scare Farm. With a theatrical booming voice proclaimed 'To the Farm'.
Although Eliza *et al* (meaning Eliza, Steve and Chloë) left straight away tummy power took control. Going straight home to #15 Eliza, Steve and Chloë were rewarded with a lunch of home cooked green eye balls and chips with rotten duck sause – Not tomato sauce, by Katie.
'So, what plans do you three have this afternoon?' enquired Katie.
'Going to walk around the swamp out back' said Eliza, who had previously warned Steve and Chloë not to divulge their true intentions of investigating the Scare Farm.
'Ok, have fun and I'm really glad you are outside in this nice weather. Take the CB with you please, they've been charged overnight'.

'Will do Mum' said Eliza as she cleared her plate in the living-room. Thinking it sucks here that mobile phones don't work, remembering zombie dad saying it's something to do with being in a tiny narrow valley, *and* a small zombie population *and* the cost of a mast.

Eliza, Steve and Chloë left via the back gate and Steve showed them the route the two zombies (dressed in heavy black clothes, the most sinister of all clothes!) took.

So three trepid investigators walked up the swamp passing the backs of cave #17, 19, 19a, 21 and 22 where they overheard Aunt Sweary living up to her name shouting, at no one in particular, about this huge zombie dog *'poo'* she stepped in. Stifling some laughter and trying to be incognito Eliza *et al* squeezed through a gap in the hedge row and ran (bent over, in a vain attempt to avoid being spotted) across the field to the dense trees/undergrowth that boarders the Scare Farm.

'This is where they went through. Here' said Steve.

Before them a narrow swamp track/path disappeared in to the dark wood. Eliza hesitated.

'Right let's follow' said Chloë as she walked in-between Steve and Eliza and began down the narrow path. Eliza (holding the CB tight in her goo slimy hand) and Steve followed.

The path led them through the wood to the fence that appeared to be circling the Scare Farm. Eliza *et al* stopped at this fence and stared in wonder; it was very new and shiny; it was 10' high; it was bent over at the top where sharp barbed wire was wrapped around it in tight circles; there were three thin lines of tiny red flashing lights running parallel along the fence at 2', 5'and 7' heights; And there were security cameras with large spot lights attached to them to scare zombies away.

Steve tapped Eliza and then Chloë and pointed at the nearest camera and what was strange is that the camera was looking in to the Scare Farm grounds not along the fence or outside.

'This is seriously weird' whispered Eliza.

'Yep' nodded Steve.

'You bet ya' whispered Chloë.

'Shhhh' hushed Steve and pointed at two zombies in the infamous sinister black clothes and a zombie in a white jacket walking in the grounds. Eliza *et al* automatically crouched down behind a tree and long grass/weeds.

'She's a zombie doctor', stated Eliza.

The three people were strolling and chatting in a friendly manner as one was tapping on a tablet while the other was twirling a nightstick or pole or something.

As they ambled closer some words were heard:

'Leucocoprinus'

'Bob'

'Subject A'

'Spore print'

'Welwitschia'

'Success factor 78.43%' 'Decurrent gill attachment'

The three zombies turned away and walked toward the main building. As they walked out of earshot on the back of the female zombie's jacket was written in bold letters Lead Mycologist.

Chloë looked at Steve 'wel-wit-sea-i?' she asked.

Steve shrugged his shoulders 'le-co-co-something?'

'Who's Bob?' asked Eliza. 'Let's follow the fence and BEEP BEEP, crackle. Eliza jumped and dropped the CB 'Eliza hon. We are going shopping in ten minutes. Can you and Steve come now please.'

Eliza picked up the CB and whispered 'yes, ok Mum'

'What?'

From inside the scare grounds a bang echoed. As if the sound were a starting pistol Eliza, Steve and Chloë stood up and ran down the path. Eliza held the CB to her mouth and managed to say 'coming home now Mum'.

'9 o'clock and all's well' cried Andre. 'Welcome to my humble abode and welcome all to the Annual Scare Berry Hunter Party'.

The collective reply consisted of various cheering, a few 'hip-hip-hoorays', the raising of glasses of swamp juice and table tapping.

'Scare! Scare! Scare!' chanted zombie Jannie and Winston. Others joined in 'Scare! Scare! Scare!' until: 'What's the matter Hip? Forgotten the words!' shouted Sparkie. While Henry just nodded and joined in. You see *when in Rome Ville*...

Lots more cheering followed by more 'Scare! Scare! Scare! So the Annual Scare Berry Hunter Party began in all its Roman pomp and glory. Often the small Berry Hunter zombie cave looked quite busy with just 7 persons, all in all doing their part time job of propping up the pub-cave. But tonight, The Berry Hunter could boast as many as 30 zombies. Although cramped and jockeying for positions at the bar and bathroom it was a happy and jolly atmosphere. Scare! Scare! Scare! Would spontaneously break out, along with the reply 'What's the matter [someone's name] forgotten the words!' There were discussions of the most ideal Scare design and Civic Crown (David's contribution) with Andre presentation of a bag of dried out rotten green brack sauce to the Best dressed Scare zombie. Also presenting two bags of brack sauce to the worst dressed zombie.

As the evening continued although some local zombies had drifted away, they were quickly replaced by a few more in hastily fashioned zombies. Then around 11.15pm the front door cave crashed open and a 5'10" stocky zombies stood proud in the doorway. For the first time that evening the Pub fell silent as every zombie focused on this new arrivals; whose bright green eyes appeared to glow; whose green inked face had a long brown smudge down one cheek; whose neck was peppered with tiny yellow dots; whose rudimentary version of David's, now infamous, Civic Crown appeared to be a circle of brambles and wire; whose dress was a little muddy and torn; whose feet were full of mud and shoeless.

'I am the Zombie King!!!'

Sunday

'Roastday' shouted David, looking at the clock above the bar that was showing 12.07am. Then realizing the zombie pub was quiet (and feeling rather stupid) David turned around to face the front door joining in a collective pause as the Scare Hunters entire clientele quickly processed this new arrival. Then...'Yeah!', 'wahoo', 'Zombie', 'Toga King' was shouted out in unison. A couple zombies hugged this new entrant, a moss drink was thrust into his oily hand and the merriment continued into the pre-dawn hours of Sunday morning.

'You're up early' said Katie as Eliza walked in to the kitchen.

'Yep Ma. What are you doing today? What roasted vermin is it today? Where Dad at?'

'Lots of early morning questions Zah. What are you after?'

'Nothin' 'hmmmm' pondered Katie 'As for your father? Did you hear him come back last night? Well this morning really?'

'Nope. Is he in trouble?'

'Let's just say next-door heard him. He tried to open #19 and when the key wouldn't fit started banging on the door yelling "whose painted the front door and locked me out" it's a good job Jakey-no-shoulders was also at that *frat party* last night too'

Eliza giggled.

'It's no laughing matter. I had to lean out of the window and shout at him to get in here' Eliza laughed even more and this time Katie joined in. Then a thud was heard and slowly David walked down the stairs. As the slow descent continued, becoming both nearer and louder Eliza said 'Uh-oh, shall I go Mum?'

'No stay here Zah, I want you to see the effects caused by alcohol.'

Philippa was outside looking at her car. Laurent Bailey was walking past on a post-drinking-wake-me-up march and waved up. Noticing she was not happy he walked over 'what's up Squeak? Wasn't last night a blast?'

'Hey Spark. This is what's up' said Philippa as she pointed at her car 'look all four tyres are flat' 'Ouch' remarked Laurent 'What on earth has happened here' and he bent down examining the tyre as if he were researching a book on tyre treads, styles, rain grooves, punctures etc. 'hmmmmm. You've got a line of holes as if you drove over one of them there zombie police stingers' 'I'd felt that' defended Philippa 'Well yeah, but I think they let the air out slowly and if it happened just down the road then perhaps the air came out over night? Perhaps?'

'Interesting theory Spark, but why put a stinger out here?

'Uhhhh-'

'Hey Pip. Hey Sparkie' shouted Henry; he walked across from his cave waving. 'Zombo, last night...Wow'

'Damn right Hip' answered a proud Laurent; 'hey to you and who the hell was calling themselves the Zombie Toga King?'

'I think it's One-shirt'.

'No way! One-shirt, he'd never let his hair down like That.'

'Well then...What about Butros' reasoned Henry

'Could be. Could be, seems the type of thing a frustrated zombie might do. Hey Hip, guess what. I crossed swords with the Zombie King and his wee was almost glowing. It was so orange. Zombo he'd been drinking some serious stuff!'

'Uhhh. What like some of Andres home brew!' grimaced Henry. Then pausing for a brief moment continued 'hang on Spark. You like looking at other zombies wee then?'

'Come off it. You can't help in a situation like that, also he were standing so close that I nearly-' 'Zombies, talking about orange wee is all-and-well.

Of course, I'd really love to listen to your debates *all day long*. But can a zombie help me get these wheels off, take me and them to town please?'

'Sure' said Laurent, shrugging his shoulders.

'I'll help too Pip. Especially for swamp grup and baked eye ball gulup?' said Henry.

'Kay Zombos. Thanks for this. I'll put on some nice Flamming swamp lankar for you'.

'What happens at the Zombie Toga party stays at the Zombie Toga party' offered David 'But this wasn't at the Zombie Toga party. Was it?' replied Katie.

'Can you argue that because it was on the way home it was connected to it and therefore part of it? ....Please?' 'Zombos [Steve had joined them as well] you see this is what happens if you drink swamp lankar, wear and ruin a damn good cotton sheet and behave like a...well a drunk' argued Katie.

'You know zombie Mum would have zombie sat last night and we both could have gone?'

'So that justifies banging on Jake's cave door and nearly breaking their lock?

Sensing he had seriously messed up. David stopped before he could make things worse. 'Sorry sweet zombie. Next year I won't go. I will stay at the cave with you'.

'No. Next year I will go and you stay in the cave. Is that clear?

'Anyway. It's Roast-day so what shall we do?'
Before anyone else could answer Eliza quickly interjected
'me, Steve and Chlo will be hanging around out back'
'OK' Said David 'Hmmmmm' said an inquisitive Katie 'just
what does this hanging around out back entail young
zombie?'
'Zombie Mum, it means hanging around out back' said
Steve.
'Yeah sure. That's fine' said David, not actually realizing
the mistrust surrounding this hanging out back issue 'What
say I look after you today Kay-dee and cook a nice rotten
down meal for all of us and you know....' Giving Katie a
mysterious wink.
'Well that will help. OK zombies you can go and *hang
around out back* and your Father can clean up.
Everywhere! Oh, and take the CB'.
Eliza and Steve left via the back of the cave and began
to follow the path back to the fence. Chloë could not
make it today as it was Roast-day and her family always
went out for a Sunday walk and roast, *at the same zombie-
pub every week*! Elissa would be doing family stuff *as well*.
Anyway, Eliza turned down the volume of the CB and
then took out of her pocket a small digital camera
'evidence' she said.
'Good one Zah' said Steve 'so...what's the plan?'
'We follow the fence around and do some investigating'
'Right-ho' answered Steve.
As they walked past #21 Steve spotted a zombie-cat
pawing at something, 'Aint that number 10's zombie-cat,
the one with the funny name?'
Eliza glanced back 'Yeah, hope it don't poo on Zombie
Dads front lawn again!'

However, as the children passed by, the zombie cat quickly jumped back, hissed and ran off with what appeared to be some Ivy caught around its collar.

Katie was in the front garden looking at her dead roses and a blur caught her eye. She watched Puss-kins-Mc-Tiny-Paws dash across the road and ran up to the front door of number 10. Killed a field mouse, thought Katie as she pruned a yellow rose. Beep Beep, 'Hi Katie' shouted Laurent as he drove past in his zombie-make-shift-van with Henry and Philippa in.

'Hello!' shouted Katie thinking what's going on there.

Back at the same spot by the fence as they were yesterday Eliza and Steve were crouched down, looking at the camera (which was pointing inside the scare farm) and listening hard. Looking down along the fence you could see that the wood had been cleared about 4 feet from the fence. Hmmm thought Eliza, it would be too obvious to walk down this part but...

'All is quiet' whispered Eliza 'Let's run along this wide bit to that tree and then hide'.

Steve nodded in agreement and both quickly ran (while crouching) along the path a small way and then crouched down behind a tree. This running/crouching and stopping continued as the intrepid investigators followed the fence, which circled the farm. Then during one pause Eliza tapped Steve and pointed to the scare farm.

Four zombies could be seen. Three zombies dressed in black and a forth with bright white hair wearing a white coat.

They did not appear as happy as yesterday. But today they were closer and Eliza and Steve could hear everything.

'So, he threw a white sheet around him and walked out of the front gate' said the white hair zombie in disbelief.

'Sir' agreed one of the zombie-guards, 'we believe he then walked down the street and in the pub, several hours later came back and started banging on the front gate -' 'Hold on a minute' interrupted the white hair zombie 'Number 1. How did he get let out? Number 2. What happened in the pub? Number 3. Why did he come back?'
'Sir.
He showed the zombie-guard a pass and walked out, I don't know what happened in the Pub cave but the cameras showed the zombie going straight there and 3 hours later came out, where he then staggered back this way! He was quite drunk indeed sir'.
'But his features? Surely that would have raised questions? Or even calls?'
'The pub was having a scare toga fancy dress party Sir'
'Damn you zombies are lucky' said a much relieved white hair zombie 'I mean damn lucky, I mean he is looking a lot better today. Perhaps the swamp lankar has helped?
'Dr Jones!'
'Ah. Professor Jennings' said the white hair zombie. Eliza and Steve watched as the zombie from yesterday ran over. You have heard about the *serious security breach* yesterday? The zombie said glaring at the three zombies.
'Yes. It appears we have had a lucky escape' answered Dr Jones.
'Agreed' said Prof Jennings 'And swamp lankar appears to be improving the situation.
Please come, I must show you this'. Prof Jennings held out a tablet and began furiously tapping on the screen, 'Look at the candle graph here and notice-' An airplane flew overhead stopping Eliza and Steve from hearing the conversation. 'Damn' said Steve as he looked at the plane wishing it would hurry up and go away. '-

Surely that's a moot point and further research is needed' stated Dr Jones.

'Do you have the time and resources for that?' questioned Prof Jennings 'Well we can do and use Doctors Baines, Thompson...NO, Parsons' 'Perhaps. Look, back to the lab' said Prof Jennings and both white coats walked off towards the main complex leaving the zombie-guards stranded like lost zombie- sheep. They stood still, quiet and sullen almost hanging their heads in shame.

'Zombie Dad was at that party' whispered Steve. Quickly Eliza snapped some pictures of the shameful zombie-guards and walking away zombies, 'Evidence' she whispered back to Steve.

'You should have filmed that' 'Movie mode do not work on this one anymore' said Eliza as she snapped a close up of the flashing lights on the fence and then of one of the many cameras.

'What now?' asked Steve, then holding out his hand 'Feel that?'

'Yep' replied Eliza it's gonna' rain big time. Let's go home'..As they turned---Steve's shoe came off.

'Hold on Zah' said Steve with a little panic in his voice. He hopped on one foot, crouched down and yanked his shoe from the undergrowth.

'Look the laces got caught up in the weeds' said Steve as he quickly slipped on his shoe. Then the run-crouch hide routine started again.

Monday

'Moanday! Moanday!' shouted Eliza while shaking Steve 'we've all overslept'.

Katie's voice drifted up the stairs 'Leave your brother alone'. Eliza ran out of Steve's room leaving Steve with happy sleepy thoughts of lying in a warm bed and not going to school.

'Stop picking on your brother young lady' said Katie

'Mum, it fun!'

'At the moment, yes. But what happens when he picks on you?'

'That will never happen Mum'..

'Oh, I think one day, perhaps when your both older –

'Zombie Mum' interjected Eliza 'At the party did Zombie Dad see a strange man?'

'Why are you asking Zah?' questioned Katie 'what's going on in that curious mind of yours?'

'Well we were up at the farm and heard them talking about someone going to the party'.

'Eliza' said Katie in a teacher type voice 'you know you shouldn't snoop around there and listen in to other people's conversations. Katie looked at Eliza 'so come on then what did you hear?'

Mary and Percy Green were coming back from their morning stroll and waved at Henry. 'Morning Henry' said Mary.

'Hey there'

'How are you?' asked Percy.

'Fine, ok. Yep. Off to work soon, I start later now to miss the rush hour traffic-'

'Ooh!' said Mary 'did you hear the traffic last night. Well this morning at 3am?'

'Nah'

'Well Percy was snoring extra loud' said Mary while looking at Percy. *'Extra Loud'* looking at Henry 'and I while we looked out the front window and saw 4 large black mini-buses slowly drive by.'

'Really?' said Henry

'Yeah. And I couldn't see inside as the windows were blacked out. I think they went in to the farm. I did notice though the headlights didn't go up the hill toward Higher Berry. I *definitely* heard the engines stop' 'Interesting' pondered Henry zombie, 'that place is getting more bizarre by the day'

'What ya mean Hip?' asked Percy zombie.

'You heard about Squeaks tyres?'

'Yeah' replied Mary zombie, 'you reckon that's all connected?'

with curiosity and adventure widening her eyes with intrigue.

'Most *definitely*' said Henry zombie, making Mary zombie's eyes widen even more 'think I'll walk by later'.

Come on Percy zombie, Henry zombie needs to go to work' said Mary zombie.

Yeah thought Henry zombie, before your eyes pop out of their sockets. Henry zombie smirked and walked over to his zombie car. He secretly loved planting intrigue into Mary zombie and Percy zombie's mind and besides it been cheeky of him he hoped it gave them a little bit of purpose. But having thought that the farm is beginning to intrigue him as well and a scare farm with such smartly dressed zombie, they *have* to be responsible for that stinger.

'That's an odd story Eliza zombie' said Katie zombie, who was sitting at the table eating some (far too healthy in Eliza zombie's opinion) ground dried worms with cut up kiwanian juice, rotten pineapple and black watermelon. Steve and David zombie also joined in. Eliza zombie and Steve zombie had explained their two trips and shown the photos to their parent-zombies.

'So, they have cameras looking at the pub cave and swamp lankar improved his situation?' said a confused David zombie. Now looking at Katie zombie 'Kay zombie this is odd! I remember that zombie?

I thought it was Butros zombie. I mean he had yellow dots on his neck and kept shouting "I am the Toga Zombie King"'.

Katie zombie leaned over and moved David zombie's chin to see both sides of his neck 'hmmmm. No yellow spots here. This isn't good at all. That scare farm is far too secretive and modern for round here'.

'You want to come and investigate with us today zombie Dad?'

Asked Ben zombie.

'No, ummm look Zah zombie and Steve zombie' said David zombie staring at his version of Katie zombie's brack sauce stew 'please can you leave running around it for today. I'm feeling all itchy 'cause of that yellow spotted neck business and the 'improved the situation' bit you said'.

'Your zombie Father is right children' contributed Katie zombie, 'anyway we were thinking of going in to town and perhaps' knowing that this will grab their attention 'going to Señor Burger for a nice meal?'

'Awww yah Mum zombie' shouted Ben zombie.

'You're the best' said Eliza zombie.

'I also agree' said David zombie Katie zombie stood up and looked proudly at her zombie family 'Right then zombies. Finish your breakfast and we will leave in 30 minutes' Chloë zombie was sitting in her room and uncomfortably full.

She shouldn't have had that Murder-by-sour-chocolaté desert from the fridge, just now. She was thinking of popping over to see Zah zombie and B zombie and perhaps they could call on L zombie as well and play some football. But at the moment her tummy felt heavy and awkward. So, taking out her telescope and looking out of the side window of her bedroom, She could see the Scare Berry Hunter and part of the road turning the corner to the scare farm. Unfortunately, she could not see much of the scare farm - Only part of a mobile phone tower and a chimney, which was lightly puffing out purple smoke.

'Purple smoke!' shouted Chloë zombie as she grabbed her phone to text Eliza zombie, 'ahhhh. No signal'. Chloë zombie looked out of her other window at number 15 'ahhh they are out'. She returned to her telescope and looked again.

No smoke. *There was purple smoke* she thought. 'There was purple smoke' she told herself out loud in an attempt to convince herself that it was an irrefutable fact. She wondered if L zombie were around and went off to number 10.

Mary zombie and Percy zombie were walking back from their investigation, which produced no results at all. Passing number 11 Laurent zombie was seen doing some bad painting to his door.

'Sparkie!' called Percy zombie.

'Hello' said Laurent zombie and moving aside from the door 'admiring my amazing work?'

'Of course,' said Mary zombie and walked over to Laurent zombie with Percy zombie following.

'So' said Mary zombie 'The zombie scare farm seems mighty strange lately?'

'Yep indeedy' said Laurent zombie 'I suspect that's something to do with that as well' pointing at the approaching large black mini bus.

All three zombies turned and watched as the large black minibus, with very dark tinted windows, so dark that you couldn't tell if any zombies was inside or even driving it.

Anyway, if a zombie vehicle could drive sinisterly then this minibus won First Place as it slowly drove by heading (presumably) to the scare farm.

Percy zombie was the first to speak 'You hear that grating sound from it', which was more of a statement rather than a question.

'Yeah' nodded Laurent zombie, 'it's got winter tyres on it' then pausing to try to comprehend the reason 'I mean why?

Seriously? Why?'

'I'm getting bad vibes about that place' said Mary zombie.

'Elissa zombie honey. Chloë zombie called out Rosie zombie. 'Come in please Chlo' zombie. Chloë zombie stepped in to the hallway with the strange flower patterned wallpaper 'Thank you Mrs. Fox' zombie she politely replied.

'No worries Chlo' zombie said Rosie zombie as Elissa zombie ran down the stairs.

'What's up Chlo zombie?' smiled Elissa zombie.

'You want to hang out today L zombie?'

'Sure'

'I want to show you something' whispered Chloë zombie, then holding Elissa zombie's arm 'Let's go outside'
'Mum' shouted Elissa zombie 'I'm going outside with Chlo' zombie.
'Ok' called out Rosie zombie, 'Be back at...errr.....four-ish'
'Ok. Bye zombie Mum' and Elissa zombie walked outside with Chloë zombie and shut the door. Straight away Chloë zombie updated Elissa zombie with the latest on the scare farm and the purple smoke incident.
'Wowzers' answered Elissa zombie, 'you know when I walked past the front gate with zombie Dad *on one of his marches* he waved and said "hello" to the guard zombie. Why don't we walk past and say "hello"'?
'Good idea L!' remarked Chloë zombie 'and-' 'Look!' snapped Elissa zombie.
A black minibus slowly drove past them. Chloë zombie and Elissa zombie watched it with utter fascination. Elissa zombie noticed that Laurent zombie, Mary zombie and Percy zombie were staring at it.
'I bet that's going to the scare farm' said Elissa zombie, 'c-mon let's follow it' Elissa zombie and Chloë zombie ran up the hill following the minibus. The minibus sped up a little and Chloë zombie and Elissa zombie soon lost sight of it. However, around the corner between number 20 and 22 both girl zombies watched the front gate of the scare farm close. Out of breath, hot and sweaty from running up the hill they stopped and began to walk slowly to the gate.
'What shall we say' said Chloë zombie.
'Just hello'
'And?'
'And they talk to us!' stated Elissa zombie. Slowly they walked up to the gate (which now appeared rather un-inviting), menacing and even unfriendly.

Standing just 3 feet away 'Hello' called out Elissa zombie
Nothing 'Hello' repeated Elissa zombie
Nothing!
'Hello!!' shouted Elissa zombie.
A large CCTV camera with glowing red spotlights under it
swiveled and looked at the zombie crew.
'This not good' whispered Chloë zombie, noticing that
Elissa zombie had stepped backwards. Probably
involuntarily. Chloë zombie stepped back to join her. The
camera wurred a little, as if it were focusing on them and
analyzing them in detail.
'Hello' said Elissa zombie, 'we... errr...want...Yes. Want to
buy some green eyed balls and worms?'
The camera continued to stare at both zombie girls.
'Anyone?' asked Chloë zombie Nothing.
'Huh!' stamped Chloë zombie, 'you are so rude!' then
grabbing Elissa zombie's arm 'we take our business
elsewhere!' and turned Elissa zombie around to walk back
to where they came.
Whispering to Elissa zombie...Chloë zombie said 'We'll get
Zah zombie and B zombie and show you the track' as they
walked towards the village.
Henry zombie returned from work and parked, making
sure he wasn't 2 inches in front of number 6. Otherwise
oneshirt zombie will moan! *Like he owns the road in front
of his house, damn turd nuffler*, thought Henry zombie. All
day long Henry zombie had been thinking of how to
investigate the scare farm, without appearing to
investigate it, and his plan was thus: I will wear some
jogging gear and jog around the fields and track behind the
opposite cave houses.

The simplest plans are the best! So, Henry zombie quickly changed and came jogging down the street heading for the track in between number 3 and 5. However Henry zombie is "NO" zombie jogger and as with so many new-years resolutioners he covered approximately 12 feet in distance before his zombie muscles started giving out. Ouch!

Thought Henry zombie as he walked across the road to the track 'Great Plan numpty' muttered Henry zombie scolding himself. Standing near the old shed rubbing his calf Henry zombie heard some tapping from the shed. From within the derelict shed. Henry zombie thought to himself... more tapping. What...From inside an abandoned shed? More tapping? Why...an old run-down shed, but with a brand new shinny door handle. More tapping? Quite strange indeed! Henry zombie walked over and tried the handle. The door opened revealing a zombie in black overalls, wearing a gas mask and holding what appeared to be a mini electric cattle prod. 'Oh' said Henry zombie. Buzzz!.........

Henry zombie looked down at his arm where he had been prodded/tasered/zapped/ whatever and looked back at the zombie and faintly said 'ow'.

The figure calmly stood back and allowed Henry zombie to collapse inside the shed.

Then the zombie gently closed the door. Slowly Henry zombie began to lose consciousness and although his eye sight was blurry he noticed bunches of wires, camera monitors, PCs, keyboards, lots of flashing lights, and a map of the village with a large red circle around it. Just as Henry zombie finally blacked out he heard a soft female zombie voice above him say 'We have suspect HS"!

Tuesday

'Booze-Day' yelled Jake zombie as he climbed in his forestry truck.

'Not on a week day JJ zombie' replied Josh zombie as he got into his car with his wife Carolyn zombie and step - zombie Elissa zombie.

'Woose!' yelled Jake zombie as he drove by in a cloud of burnt diesel fumes honking the horn five times and waving madly out the window.

'JJ zombie's rather happy this morning' said Julian zombie turning towards Carolyn zombie....

'Mmm' replied Carolyn zombie...

'Mum, Josh zombie what time will we be back? Can I hang out with Zah zombie and co later today?'

'One-ish Elissa zombie. Is that ok with your plans?' relied Carolyn zombie.

Elissa zombie sank back in the car seat, 'guess it will have to do' she huffed!

Meanwhile by the rear hedgerow of the large back garden of number 21 Sebastian zombie was weeding and wishing he still had his old rotavator to churn up a nice rotten vegetable patch for himself. But that would be a lot of work, although nice rewarding work he thought as he tried to loosen a particularly stubborn weed.

'Nearly... there' winced Sebastian zombie as he shook the weed. When suddenly two tiny tendrils wrapped themselves around his wrist. Sebastian zombie watched in stunned silence and horror as the two tiny vines began withering around his wrist becoming tighter and tighter. He quickly snapped out of his amazement and jerked his arm backwards while pulling at the vines with his free hand. He pulled at one of the vines and it snapped near the root and the other loosened straight away going limp and finally sliding off his wrist.

28

'What the...' he muttered to himself in an astonished voice. Holding up the first vine he stared at it thinking that didn't happen. Did it? No bloody way matey. That shouldn't happen. Turning it over in the sunlight he noticed tiny hair length thorns on the vine and then held up his arm to reveal a line of tiny pinpoints of blood. Sebastian zombie walked back to his kitchen and poured water on his arm leaving the snapped vine on his countertop.

'What the' he repeated to himself again as he continued pouring cold water over his arm.

Everyone had met at the back of Eliza zombie's house as her Zombie parents had told both Eliza zombie and Ben zombie to stay away from the scare farm. But of course, in reality that meant please go and investigate the scare farm as-soon-as-possible.

So, this time Eliza zombie and Ben zombie had a backpack with some rotten-chocolate bars, swamp water, two CB's and a camera. So at 1.30pm Eliza zombie, Ben zombie, Chloë zombie and Elissa zombie (Eliza *et al*) set off investigating.

'Purple smoke!' exclaimed Ben zombie

'Yes I am 110% certain' said Chloë zombie

'Things are getting more weird' remarked Eliza zombie

'Very, Very, weird' agreed Elissa zombie

So off they walked with Eliza zombie explaining to all the zombies the run-crouch-hide strategy and about the flashing fence and cameras.

Back at the vine grabbing location Sebastian zombies was staring at the hedgerow looking for movement. Did the weed he had loosened reaffirmed itself in the ground and is smirking at him in a manner only weeds can?

He thought to himself. But then plants don't attack zombies, although Darwinism zombie... Perhaps a giant Venus fly trap could, especially if I sat on it! ...Sebastian zombie shook his head and thought I'll go tangled in the undergrowth so he poured some weed killer on it and heard some rustling. He froze, staring at the weed. Had it moved?

Had it tried to shake off the poison?

Looking up to see Eliza zombie, Ben zombie, Chloë zombie and Elissa zombie walking down the rudimentary track Sebastian zombie thought your mind is old and playing tricks on you as he smiled and waved at them thinking to be young and carefree! But hey I have food in my fridge older than them! The zombie strolled over to his garden bench, sat down and nursed a cold swamp lankar drink. Ben zombie waved at Santa zombie and carried on following the others until he kicked something by accident. Clink! The group stopped as Ben zombie bent down and picked up a small coin. Examining and turning it over in his fingers.

'What's it say?' demanded Eliza zombie.

'I'm getting to that Zah zombie.'

'C-mon' laughed Elissa zombie

'Yeah. C-mon' repeated Eliza

'Shut it you lot! ...Right..errr...Republic of Na-mib-ah, Nam-b-er, Na-mib-b-ah'

Chloë zombie looked over his shoulder at the coin

'Yeah...Namibia... I think' and then pointing at the coin proudly saying '2010, so it hasn't been here long'

'Where is that? And, and how did it get here!' said an excited Eliza zombie, 'quick look around here.

See if there are any more' and the four zombies began lightly kicking the dirt on the track with their shoes looking for more foreign coins.

Katie zombie was waiting outside her front door looking at her watch when she spotted Mary zombie and Percy zombie walking up from their cave house, 'Hey there' she called out waving at the same time. Mary and Percy zombie waved and began to walk over and Katie zombie walked down her front garden path to meet them at the roadside.

'How are you...and your zombie family Kay zombie?' asked Mary zombie.

'Oh fine, fine, can't complain. And yourselves?'

'Besides snoring and gurgling as loud as a ships airhorn' looking at Percy zombie 'things are spot-on'.

'I have a cold' mumbled an embarrassed Percy zombie.

'Yeah. For 20 years!' laughed Mary zombie.

'Ok...' answered Katie zombie, 'have you seen the Mobile Grocer today?'

'Yeah. It's down there' said Percy zombie pointing down the hill towards Lower Berrywood.

'Ok'...

'No. Not Ok. It appears to have four flat tyres. It's blocking the lane and everything' remarked Percy zombie 'Damn'..

'Yep just like Pip zombie's car' said Marcy zombie 'Sorry?'

'You haven't heard' said Mary zombie and pausing dramatically.

'Heard what?' answered Katie zombie (which was precisely the answer Mary zombie wanted).

Mary zombie looked around then slowly bent forward and continued in a hushed conspiracy tone of voice, 'Pip zombie's car had four flat tyres the other day. Strange, isn't it? I reckon it's to-doing with the scare farm' 'Could be' said Katie zombie, thinking I really need to get a move on here, 'look how far down is it? I need some rotten veggies'.

'Not far, a fit lady like you can easily make it there and back' said Percy zombie.

'Percy zombie!' shouted Mary zombie and she lightly hit his arm.

All three laughed, and separated. Katie zombie strolled down the hill toward the stranded Grocery van thinking that is odd, things are definitely odding up here. Is odding a word? Well it is now!

After a quick coinless search, the four zombie Middle Berrywood Investigators continued their journey to the circling fence. Eliza zombie strongly took the lead followed by Chloë zombie, Elissa zombie and Steve zombie at the back (who was still looking at the ground in random places for coins).

As they drew near the fence Eliza zombie crouched down and beckoned the others to follow suit, 'there's the fence and cameras' she whispered pointing at the tiny flashing lights and then two different cameras which were both pointing inside the compound.

'Ohhh' quietly exclaimed Elissa zombie, 'I see...'

After a brief pause that set the tone for their covert operation 'Right everyone...now' ordered Eliza zombie and she quickly ran down (parallel to the fence) to a large tree. The other three joined her, together they crouched motionless listening for anything/everything. Some low rustling sounds could be heard behind them, but that was just the breeze in the trees. Isn't it?

They continued to the next tree and the next and around the corner to where they had heard yesterday's party conversation.

Ben zombie looked around 'Nothing' he said dis-heartedly and looked up the path, 'shall we carry on Zah zombie?' 'oh yes' said Eliza zombie, pointing at another tree, 'c-mon' and she was gone with the others following. The run-crouch-hide routine continued until they had circled around the scare farm and came out on the road going up to Higher Berrywood.

'No luck today' puffed Chloë zombie.

'Except my coin' said Ben zombie as he flicked it in the air and clumsy caught it again.

'Let's double back' said Eliza zombie, and wait this 'Afternoon' Eliza zombie spun round and all four took an involuntary step back as before them was a tall zombie guard dressed in a very *sinister* looking black jumpsuit wearing a helmet with a small camera attached to it. The zombie guard had a large black (presumably) zombie guard dog on a tight leash with him.

'What yah doing?' nervously asked zombie Elissa.

'Nothing' replied the guard, '*What yah doing?*' repeated the zombie guard in an emotionless tone.

'Nothin' replied Elissa zombie.

'Good' said the zombie guard.

'Good' said Elissa zombie.

'Excuse me fellow zombies' said the zombie guard. Eliza zombie *et al* stood apart and the zombie guard and zombie dog walked down the path they came from.

The zombies watched as the zombie guard slowly strolled down the path allowing the zombie dog to stop and sniff various small plants.

'Shall we walk back?' suggested Eliza zombie.

'Yep', 'uh-huh', 'good plan' were the replies and were the replies she wanted to hear.

Returning from the stranded *Not very* Mobile Grocer Katie zombie was not thinking about the rotten veg soup and stew she had been planning but was thinking about the scare farm, Eliza zombie's tales and pictures, the zombie toga king at the party and now the punctures. Katie zombie decided that this scare farm was indeed becoming very suspicious.

Katie zombie also decided to have a good look at Dave zombie's neck tonight, and perhaps nip up to the Berry Hunter to listen to some zombie gossip.

A well-hidden and good quality CCTV camera was zooming in and focusing on the road directly outside number 4. There was a small crack in the road surface, which looked rather recent. The camera zoomed in more and a small tendril slowly emerged (approx. 4 inches long) and started prodding the road surface, two others quickly joined it and the prodding continued. The Mobile Grocer drove past (a bit too fast considering there may be zombies on the road) and the plant froze. The three tendrils began prodding again until a zombie cat walked up to it very hesitantly. Again the plant froze. The zombie cat hissed at the three tendrils. The plant bent backwards then all three tendrils shot outwards and attempted to grab the zombie cat. One went for the leg and two went for the neck.

But the zombie cat was quicker and leaped out of the way running off up the hill, presumably to the relative safety of his zombie owner's home.

The CCTV camera watched as the plant began its prodding again and a forth tendril peaked it's stem out. A zombie began feverishly typing and said 'Village Observatory here. We have a little problem'.

Wednesday

'Choppin Day Chloë zombie' said Julian zombie, 'Well I wish it were Chlo zombie, but cause it's half term Kempo is cancelled as the school is locked up. So...' with a pleading look on his face, 'So...'Chloë zombie hesitated slightly, 'Yesss zombie Dad?'

'Shall we do some kick boxing on the punch bag?'

'Why not!'

'Great, ten minutes?'

'Yep' replied Chloë zombie who ran upstairs to get changed.

Just after Chloë zombie was changing in to her *choppin* gear she picked up her telescope and looked towards the scare farms chimney, 'fudge! No smoke'.

'Chlo zombie' called Julian zombie 'I am going out there now' 'zombie Kay Dad' And now, thought Chloë zombie, I can punch and kick that bag like I am fighting off those menacing zombie guards, and shouting 'get ready for some Buccaneer-Bashin' she dashed down the stairs two at a time.

Having decided that zombie gossip from a cave-pub in the evening (especially during happy hour) would not yield anything other than slurry zombie songs and rude limericks Katie zombie thought she'd go on Wednesday morning when the cave-pub becomes the village post office and bank for 3 hours. And to be honest Katie zombie enjoyed doing some banking or posting letters in a bar as the atmosphere was more relaxed and genuine.

'Hello Kay zombie' said Isabel the cave-pub land zombie/bank manager/post zombie/general zombie guru and fountain of all local knowledge and gossip.

'Hey Issy zombie'.

'What's it today?'

'One letter to Kramfors, Sweden please and…. All the latest information you have on the Scare Farm' stated Katie zombie.

Isabel zombie's eyes widen, 'Really? Well then as you're me only customer at the mo, sit down over there and I'll get some coffee'.

Returning from an amazing punching and kicking session Chloë zombie was ready to collapse on her bed, too exhausted to jump in the shower. But first I'll have a quick peak at the chimney.

She lifted up her telescope feeling her arm muscles wince (she had overdone and zombie Dad had told her to calm down several times, but secretly she could tell that he was impressed) and looked out. Nothing, but as she panned to the right viewing part of the field adjacent to number 20 her mouth dropped open. She was watching a small dust devil approximately 6ft high spinning madly and moving slowly across the field to her right, it was bright yellow spinning small pieces of vines and leaves around it and tossing them in the air.

'Oh…Mmm…Geee', Chloë zombie uttered as she followed the dust devil's path until bang! The telescope hit the side of her window and the dust devil moved out of her line of sight. Chloë zombie dropped the telescope and ran downstairs heading towards Eliza zombie's and Steve zombie's house.

Banging on the door and at the same time bending down to lift up the letterbox Chloë zombie urgently shouted through the rusty rectangle mouth 'Zah! B,… Zah'. From within she heard 'hang-on'.

'Quicker. Quicker. Quicker!' Chloë zombie shouted back through the open letterbox.

The door opened. Chloë zombie grabbed Eliza zombie,
'Quick. Run...
Now' she ordered while pulling Eliza zombie down the
front garden path.
'What Chlo zombie?' said a resistant Eliza zombie.
Stopping in the road and pausing to gather her breathe
Chloë zombie managed to say, 'The field' 'Blue smoke!'
exclaimed Eliza zombie.
'No'
'White coats? Zombie Guards? Zombie Sniffer dogs?'
Still breathing heavily, 'No' 'What!!' demanded Eliza
zombie.
'A tornado' Eliza zombie didn't even reply, she turned and
bolted up the hill as if she were sprinting the Olympic
100metre final.
Chloë zombie exhaled deeply, turned and followed.
'Wow' shouted Eliza zombie as they were running up the
hill.
'Wow...how big...'
'Like... taller than.... Zombie Dad....'
'Wow'
'And it's... yellow'
'Wow, wow...wow'
Katie zombie left the Scare Berry Hunter feeling rather
perplexed but couldn't decide if it was in a good or bad
way. As she closed the door, Eliza zombie and Elissa
zombie both ran past.
'Hey Mum'
'Zah!'
'Bye zombie Mum'
'What you up to young zombie?'
'Nothing' called back Eliza zombie.
'Yes' called back Chloë zombie.

'Be careful and don't go snooping' shouted Katie zombie, but she doubted they heard that over their heavy pounding and breathing running up the hill.

Tony zombie was yawning very loudly as he walked toward his car in the distinctive management uniform of the distinctive large super market chain and noticed the Greenies walking toward him.

'You're often up in the wee morning hours Mary zombie' Tony zombie stated rather than asked.

'Well she's a light sleeper' said Percy zombie before Mary zombie could reply.

Looking at Percy zombie, Mary zombie said 'yes...that's right... A *very* light sleeper'.

'Did you see anything odd last night? Well this morning really?'

'Slept through last night'.

Percy zombie smugly smiled.

'Which is a rarity' continued Mary zombie, still looking at Percy zombie, whose smile then disintegrated.

'Anyway' said Tony zombie, 'Last night.

Well this morning at about 3.30 I parked here and looked up the street to see a zombie truck in the road and three zombies walking very slowly in front of it'.

'Ohhhh' exclaimed Mary zombie, 'And...'

'And.... And.... they were walking down the hill toward me while spraying stuff on the road. I stood here and watched them. One of them noticed me and waved'.

'What a get-lost-wave or happy-wave?' asked Percy zombie (who felt a little left out of the conversation).

'Happy wave'

'And...' urged Mary zombie.

'And then wrote on a white board and held it up. It said "weed control" Then he rubbed that message off and wrote "night shift"'

'Weed control! Weed control here, at 3.30 in the morning!'

'Yeah'

'Ohhh...That's suspicious'

'And it gets a little more suspicious' replied Tony zombie. Marcy zombie grabbed his arm, 'Tell me!'

'They had two dogs with them sniffing the kerb edges. Then when a dog sat down one of the men went over and sprayed some weed killer'

'Dogs sniffing for weeds!' shouted Mary zombie, 'Why?'

'Ha!' laughed Tony zombie, 'Yeah dogs sniffing for greenery!'

'Not that sort of weed' said Mary zombie, 'I doubt we have wild grass growing up and down here!'

'What about Hip zombie' stated Percy zombie.

'Percy zombie!' scolded Mary zombie, 'So what else Tony zombie?'

'Well, I felt weird stood there watching them so went inside and spied on them out of my front bedroom. All they did was go down the street spraying the kerb side, especially where one of the dogs sat down'

'Where?' asked Mary zombie in a demanding tone.

'Just there' said Tony zombie pointing at a shriveled plant.

'Ohh' and Mary (with Percy zombie following) walked over to investigate.

'In this field' said Chloë zombie standing next to a field that was covered in grass about say 3 feet high. 'Look, there is a path here' pointed Eliza zombie.

Both zombies looked at the slightly depressed grass track running its way across the field.

The track was also lightly speckled with snapped pieces of grass and other plants. 'Let's follow it' said Eliza zombie beginning to walk along it while looking down at the snapped-off pieces of long grass and other weeds/plants.
'Look' said Chloë zombie who had stopped and was kicking a small withered tendril approximately 12 inches long, 'it's got lots of yellow dots on it'.
Both zombies bent down and examined the tendril (but without touching it).
'Oh yeah' agreed Eliza zombie and then looked around at the depressed grass 'there's lots of yellow dots all over the place.'
'And on our shoes' said Chloë zombie holding up her trainer.
'Ohhh. That's not good'
'It was a yellow tornado' exclaimed Chloë zombie in a matter-of-the-fact voice.
'Yes' agreed Eliza zombie. So, both zombies followed the depressed grass track making sure they didn't touch anything.
'Wish I had the camera' said Eliza zombie.
'Yeah then-'
'Brack sauce!'
Both zombies froze and could see some rustling in the trees ahead.
'Quick! Hide' ordered Eliza zombie and both zombies ran off the depressed grass track and hid in the long grass. As they were hiding they realized they couldn't see anything but heard:
'Yes. Yes, you're the Zombie Toga King'
'I am the Zombie Toga King. And you will love my-'
'Yes yes, ok.'
'Settle down now.'
'Brack sauce!'

'Ok then. We are going back now for a cup of tea.'
'Brack sauce!'
Chloë zombie looked up and tapped Eliza zombie, 'Quick. I bet they are going back to the farm' and both zombies ran over to the path to see...to see... to see the large black gate of the scare farm firmly close.
'Ahhhh' shouted Eliza zombie and stamped her feet, 'C-mon L.
I'm telling zombie Mum' and both zombies headed down the hill.
Katie zombie noticed Mary zombie and Percy zombie staring at a dead plant, 'What's up? She asked.
'Sinister things are up!' replied Mary zombie, 'or dead!' pointing to the withered weed and then explained and exaggerated her conversation with Tony zombie.
'Now I am concerned about that farm' said Katie zombie, 'things are indeed odd up there' pointing towards the hill. Seeing Eliza zombie and Chloë zombie returning from the hill.
'Zombie Mum! Zombie Mum' shouted Eliza zombie, 'Listen to this!'
Not wanting an audience Katie zombie said 'inside then zombies and we'll have fried caterpillars and swamp juice!'
Katie zombie followed along with Eliza zombie and Chloë zombie leaving Mary and Percy zombie examining the dead weed.
'Puss-kins!' called Rosie zombie, 'Puss-kinnns'
Nothing.
Standing on her front gate, Rosie zombie wasn't embarrassed calling for the strangely named Puss-kins-McTiny-Paws and in fact thought that the unusual name gave the zombie cat a top feline status.

She's heard other neighbors calling the name and stroking the ginger-tom as well as giving it a treat. But still it was after 11 in the evening.

Walking to the front gate Rosie zombie called again, 'Pusskins!

Dinner, your favourite'. Nothing.

Rosie zombie walked back to the door thinking where can Pusskins be, she's rarely this late for dinner. Just before Rosie zombie closed the door she called out a final time: 'Pussssss-Kinnnnnns'

Thursday

'Firsday' said David zombie to Eliza zombie over their brack sauce surprise with zombie swamp lankar today!

'Don't really count zombie Dad. As it's half term'

'It counts to the 9-5 workers!'

'Suppose so' mumbled Eliza zombie.

'Please don't go near that Farm or anyone shouting about how they are a Zombie Toga King.'

'No Dad, you can trust me'

'Hmmmmm', then turning to face Katie zombie, 'I'll be out all day at the Smithy job'

'Kay zombie hon'

'zombie Mum, zombie Dad. Honestly now. We won't go up to the Farm. Ben zombie and I will meet L zombie at the field and play some football'

'Please do just that Zah zombie. I am getting some bad vibes from that place. And please please take your CB with you.'

'Sure zombie Mum' and off ran Eliza zombie to get ready for *football*.

David zombie looked at Katie zombie, 'Do you think any football will be played?'

Katie zombie looked back at David zombie, 'What do you think?'

So, our four zombie investigators meet at the field to play football. Eliza zombie looked at her fellow group members (Chloë zombie, Elissa zombie and Steve zombie) and standing in a theatrical pose, 'Right then' she commanded, 'we run across there' pointing to the shed 'And up behind the cave houses to the farm. OK?'

There was a collective agreement and the plan was put in to immediate action.

Across the road from Eliza *et al* Percy zombie was looking
at a small crack in the plaster on the side their small (yet
cosy) bungalow. He pushed his finger in it to check the
depth and it went in quite far. Not good, I'll patch this
up today he thought as he heard the four zombies ran
past his cave house and between the old shed. He turned
around just to see them disappear around the corner
(presumably) running up the track behind the cave houses.
He turned to the crack and froze. Sticking out of the
crack were three tendrils, all withered and two stems
had leaves on them.
'That...wasn't...here...just now' the zombie said out loud,
followed by 'Mary zombie'
'Percy zombie. What is it?'
'Mary zombie. Dear. Please come here'
Mary zombie walked around from the back garden and
Percy zombie pointed at the plant sticking out of the wall,
'look'....
'How?.........What?..........Why?'
'I know' replied Percy zombie and to their horror all three
tendrils shot outwards, wrapped around Percy zombie's
finger and wrist and pulled him to the crack and his
entangled finger disappeared inside. Another two tendrils
wrapped themselves around Percy zombie's wrist and
started heading up his arm.
'Ahh' screamed Mary zombie and ran over and grabbed
Percy zombie's arm. Percy zombie grabbed his arm with
his free hand and both pulled back.
'Owwww' said Percy zombie, 'Keep pulling' (snapping
sounds) were heard. Finally, his finger came out
covered in more tangled plant tendrils and pinpoints of
blood.

Holding his finger up, 'Ow!' said Percy zombie in a complete state of shock! Mary zombie grabbed his arm and marched inside.

'Quick run cold water over your hand, and keep those plants! I'm calling the hospital, the zombie police, everyone!'

stated Mary zombie.

Running cold water over his finger untangling the plant vines, 'ow' the zombie repeated still in a state of shock'

'Percy zombie!!!' shouted Mary zombie, 'The telephone doesn't work' Rosie zombie and Josh zombie were watching zombie Puss-Kins dreaming.

'Must have come back late last night or this morning?' said Josh zombie.

'Yep. Must have had a run-in with something?'

Zombie Puss-kins was dreaming big time! Rosie zombie and Josh zombie watched her little paws and legs twitch madly whilst at the same time hissing and showing her teeth.

Rosie zombie bent down slowly and pulled a tiny piece of vine from under her collar and casually tossed it in the bin.

'Poor little thing' said Josh zombie, 'still she's safe and home now'.

'Yes, extra tuna tonight for you' said Rosie zombie.

'Thanks!' laughed Josh zombie, 'Although rotten horseradish Tuna steaks for all of us tonight?'

Running and crouching Eliza *et al* ran past the rear gardens of all the cave houses very quickly, especially number 15! They made it (probably unseen) to the path, which will take them to the Scare Farm's fence.

'I wanna see this yellow tornado' said Steve zombie.

'Me too' joined in Elissa zombie.

'I want to see this Zombie Toga King' said Eliza zombie.
Reaching the edge of the dense woodland/undergrowth
and the gap between it and the shiny flashing fence
Eliza zombie et al all instinctively crouched down and
listened for anything. Nothing. So, a repeat of the run-
crouch-hide strategy was implemented. Just before the
fourth start Ben zombie held out his arms to block Eliza
zombie, 'Zah zombie' he whispered and pointed in the
compound. A zombie in a yellow robe was walking and
being flanked by two zombie guards. Eliza *et al* watched
transfixed as the yellow robe zombie stopped to casually
sniff a flower and then sniffed the air. Then began walking
towards them.
'Can that zombie smell us?' whispered Chloë zombie.
'Perhaps Steve zombie!' joked Eliza zombie.
'But hey-'
'Brack sauce!' shouted the yellow robed zombie.
'Calm down zombie' said one of the zombie guards in an
unconcerned manner.
'Brack sauce!' Shouted the yellow robed zombie and
slowly raised his arms up in the air. As he lifted his arms up
a cloud of blades of grass, twigs and fallen leaves lifted
the zombie and began swirling around him.
'He's the tornado!' said a wide-eyed flabbergasted
Eliza zombie.
Both zombie guards were unprepared and got knocked flat
by the swirling storm of grass, twigs, and leaves.
'I am the Zombie Toga King' bellowed the, now revelled
to be Zombie Toga King, and looking up in to the sky he
exhaled a cloud of yellow dust. This dust quickly joined
in the swirling mess surrounding the Zombie Toga King
and he continued walking toward Eliza *et al* and
looking directly at them and smiling insanely shouting
'I am the Zombie Toga King, love my spores.'

Sebastian zombie was sat on his front bench today hoping that Mary zombie and Percy zombie would walk past as he wanted a chat and update of zombie village affairs. Sitting on his bench day dreaming about nothing in particular Sebastian zombie was watching the day drift by when he noticed what appeared to be a hairy football rolling down the hill. He stared at it thinking that's a tumbleweed, here, in Berrywood?

'Tumbleweed' he said to himself in a disbelieving tone. He watched it roll down past the Berry Hunter and stopped. Then rolled a bit more stopping outside number 14. Standing up to get a better view the zombie walked over to his front gate and watched as the tumbleweed appeared to have turned itself around and headed back up the hill. Yes, going up the hill! And heading towards him!

The zombie stepped back as the tumbleweed sped up, suddenly it then bounced itself into the air and flew straight at his head. Sebastian zombie hesitated in awe and finally instinct took over and he began to raise his arms to block his face. But he was too late the tumbleweed engulfed his face with tendrils and vines wrapping around his neck.

Sebastian zombie collapsed on his front garden and laid there twitching as the vines crept their way down his arms, back, chest and legs. While some tendrils pushed their way into his month and down his throat.

Chloë zombie shifted backwards first and Ben zombie joined her.

'Peg it' shouted Elissa zombie.

'Damn right, now we-'

Buzzz! And the Zombie Toga King collapsed. And the yellow tornado/swirling mess around the zombie collapsed instantly as well, leaving yellow dots everywhere.

'Took us by surprise then Dr Roberts zombie' said one of the zombie guards.

Standing over the Zombie Toga King, 'He's getting stronger' said the other zombie guard.

'Not good' replied the first zombie guard.

The Zombie Toga King wiggled slightly and as the zombie guards gently pulled him up, tilted his head toward Eliza *et al*, 'you will love my spores'.

Mary zombie decided to go next door to number 1 to use their telephone, 'Percy zombie I'm going next door'.

No reply.

'Percy zombie, I'm going next door' repeated Mary zombie harshly as she looked in the kitchen to check on Percy zombie.

'Percy zombie I said-'

Mary zombie froze.

Percy zombie stood in the middle of the kitchen with what looked like a huge wig of vines/leaves/tendril's wrapped around his head. Mary zombie could see other vines wrapped around his hands and feet as well.

'Per....'

'Love the spores' said Percy zombie in an emotionless voice.

'Per....' Said Mary zombie, now seeing large cracks on the kitchen floor with thick twitching vines coming out.

There were vines wrapped around the fridge, coming out of the oven and crawling up the walls and along the ceiling. 'Per....'

'Love the spores' said Percy zombie as two thick vines wrapped around Mary zombie's ankles while a bundle of vines dropped on her head quickly engulfing her.

'Peg it now' shouted Elissa zombie as she ran back the way they came abandoning the run-crouch-hide strategy.

All the others quickly followed.

'We have to tell zombie Mum everything' shouted Steve zombie.

'Yeah' puffed Eliza zombie, 'But I've dropped my camera'.

'Doesn't matter' said Steve zombie as the four crossed the field and passing the rear garden of Sebastian zombie's cave slowed down to a fast walk.

Returning home via the back gate all four entered the kitchen, 'zombie Mum' shouted Steve zombie.

'zombie Mum' copied Eliza zombie.

'Hello Children' said Katie zombie holding the family's landline, 'Hi L zombie and Chlo zombie' and then shaking the telephone, 'Phone network down *again*!'

Eliza zombie looked at Steve zombie, 'it must be connected!'

'Connected to what?' asked Katie zombie, 'You've been at that Farm again. Look it's not right up there-'

'I know zombie Mum' interrupted Eliza zombie.

Katie zombie sighed, 'Sit down and tell me everything'.

And, over some fried snails and swamp juice they did tell everything. In the meantime, David zombie had returned and was duly updated with all the events and as it was getting on their nerves Katie zombie and David zombie decided that tomorrow they will actually go up to the Scare Farm and demand to see the owner.

Elissa zombie and Chloë zombie left the house and waved bye to each other. Elissa zombie ran across the road to her home.

She unlocked the front door and walked inside, 'zombie Mum, zombie Dad, Eva zombie!' she called.

No answer.

'zombie Mum, Dad, Eva!' Elissa zombie repeated with panic rising in her voice.

No answer.

Elissa zombie put her hand on the door, 'zombie
Mum...zombie Dad...E....'
she whimpered.
'psst' said Rosie zombie quietly, 'shhhhh. Zombie Puss-kins
is having a mad dream again. Come and watch a sec'
'Phew' said Elissa zombie and followed her zombie Mum.
'Are you Ok L?' asked Rosie zombie quietly as they
watched Zombie Puss-kins hiss and kick at unseen enemies
in her sleep.
'Yes, zombie Mum, but I must tell you about the Farm'
'Over some rotten horse radish tuna steaks?' whispered
Josh zombie.

Friday

'Funtag' said Andre zombie as he walked down the steps to the cellar to check the beer lines.

'Funtag' he repeated to himself and opened the door to the cellar.

But it was not his cellar. It was a tropical rain forest. Andre zombie stood in utter amazement as before him were vines, tendrils and leaves covering everything and more vines as thick as rope dangling from the ceiling. The zombie could just about make out the outline of the barrels, some had been knocked over and even burst, but all were covered in a thick hairy carpet of vines, leaves and mushrooms. Indeed, there was a white mushroom in front of him about 3 foot high and just as wide.

Andre zombie closed the door and held up three fingers, 'Three' he said, and opened the door again to reveal the same tropical scene. With a deep sigh the zombie closed it again and held up four fingers. There was a thud as something hit the door from within the tropical cellar. Immediately Andre zombie spun around ran up the stairs shouting 'Issy zombie! Issy zombie!'

'Funtag' said Katie zombie.

'I hope it's a fun day and everything at that Farm is as innocent as me!' replied David zombie.

'If that Farm is as innocent as you then we're in deep trouble.'

Katie zombie and David zombie continued their walk up the hill toward the Farm, passing the Berry Hunter and then Sebastian zombie's cave. Noticing that his front door was open David zombie said 'Santa zombie's out and he knows you're looking at Katie zombie in a cheeky manner 'You've been a very naughty zombie!'

'That's all you think about isn't it!'

'Yeah. So?'

Shaking her zombie head, 'What did I do wrong to end up with you' laughed Katie zombie.

'You did nothing wrong. You won the lotto!' and they arrived at the gate to the Farm. Katie zombie walked up and knocked gently (yet firmly) on the large black metal gate.

'Zah zombie, this is a bad idea' said Steve zombie

'I need that camera' argued Eliza zombie, 'It's got pictures of the zombie toga king and he's blowing out the yellow stuff.'

'It's still a bad idea.'

'But zombie Mum and zombie Dad will definitely believe us then.'

'They already do.'

'I didn't' said Eliza zombie in her matter-of-fact voice, 'Look Steve zombie I am just going to run up and get the camera and run straight back, please come with me?'

'Kay Zah zombie.'

Elissa zombie was also convinced her zombie parents didn't believe her. Otherwise they'd gone over to Zah zombie's zombie parents *or* driven off to lower Berrywood to call the zombie police *or* up to the Farm to bang on the gate. Not waiting until today to *talk to Eliza zombie's Mum!* 'Huh!'

huffed Elissa zombie. She walked in to the zombie family bathroom to clean her teeth and turned on the tap.

Instead of water there was a strange gurgling sound and the tap began to shake rather violently.

'Zombie Mum! zombie Dad!' shouted Elissa zombie and she was lucky as Josh zombie was waiting outside so he could use it.

'What's wrong L zombie?' Josh zombie asked as Elissa zombie opened the door for him.

'Look' she said while pointing at the tap.

53

Both Josh zombie and Elissa zombie watched the shaking gurgling tap.

'Airlock!' said Josh zombie and approached the tap.

The tap ceased moving and then spat out a lump of thick brown/yellow mud and a thin tendril shot out of it and began moving in the air as if sniffing it.

'What...' said Josh zombie. The tendril stopped moving.

'What...' repeated Josh zombie and the tendril appeared to bend toward the source of the noise (being Josh zombie) and slowly twitching.

Josh zombie pulled Elissa zombie out of the way and moved her behind him. The tendril twitched again. Josh zombie kicked off his old worn slipper and it slid across the floor. The tendril shot downward and another one popped out of the tap and followed it. Both tendrils wrapped around the slipper lifting it up, pulling it back toward the tap where a third thicker vine squeezed its way out to wrap itself around the slipper as well. Then the slipper appeared to be spat out, landing back on the floor. Josh zombie slammed the bathroom door.

'We're leaving!' he said to Elissa zombie, 'Katie zombie, we have to go'.

No answer.

Katie zombie knocked again.

No answer. But this time the large CCTV camera moved around to focus on them. Feeling a little embarrassed and annoyed Katie zombie went to knock again and- A siren began wailing *Honk, Honk, Honk........Honk, Honk, Honk......Honk, Honk, Honk*

Katie zombie jumped backwards and stared at David zombie, 'errrr....'

David zombie was looking at the emotionless camera, 'I
think-'Honk, honk, honk and then over a loud tannoy
system in a clipped female South African accent *'Attention
Please. Emergency. All personnel evacuate immediately.
You have 5 minutes to reach Site Bravo'* followed by *Honk,
Honk, Honk......Honk, Honk, Honk* Katie zombie and David
zombie stared at each other and David zombie said,
'I think-'
'I think we better-'
The door slid open and 3 large black minibuses drove
out at high speed heading down the hill. Looking inside
the compound Katie zombie and David zombie watched as
zombies were running to other busses while some zombies
were hitting balls of weeds with baseball bats and pieces
of wood and one zombie appeared to be tasering one.
'This is not a scare farm' stated Katie zombie.
*'Attention Please. Emergency. All personnel evacuate
immediately. You have 4 minutes to reach Site Bravo'*
followed by *Honk, Honk, Honk......Honk, Honk, Honk.*
'Quick' said David zombie as he urgently grabbed Katie
zombie's hand, 'Let's get Zah zombie and Steve zombie
and make like a tree!'
They ran down the hill with another two minibuses
speeding past them. As they ran past the Berry Hunter
they spotted Andre zombie and Isabel zombie standing
outside.
*'Attention Please. Emergency. All personnel evacuate
immediately. You have 3 minutes to reach Site Bravo'*
echoed across the village.

'Our car keys are inside, can we come with you'
shouted Andre zombie 'Yes!' called out Katie zombie and
the four of them ran down to number 5.
'Here it is!' said Eliza zombie
'Brilliant, let's go home'
'Ok Steve zombie'
'Ok' repeated Steve zombie impatiently, 'Let's go-'
A siren shattered the urgent conversation between Eliza
zombie and Steve zombie.
'Attention Please. Emergency. All personnel evacuate
immediately. You have 5 minutes to reach Site Bravo'
followed by *Honk, Honk, Honk......Honk, Honk, Honk*
'Oh fudge' said Eliza zombie in a quiet scared tone. Staring
through the now brightly red flashing fence Eliza zombie
and Steve zombie watched guards and white-coats run
around, some had vines on their hands or feet while
another zombie was hitting a ball of weeds with a chair.
A tree inside the compound began to shake and a huge
mushroom (the size of a car!) pushed it's way out of the
ground, uprooting the tree, which fell smashing part of
the fence. Spotting the zombie guards and white-coats
running thru it and into the undergrowth passing the
children.
'Attention Please. Emergency. All personnel evacuate
immediately. You have 4 minutes to reach Site Bravo'
'Run!' shouted a white coat zombie as he ran past shaking
his arm wildly as it was engulfed in vine tendrils.
'Eliza zombie! Steve zombie' shouted a voice.
'Hip!' called Steve zombie, 'Over here' Henry zombie came
running over, 'Are you ok?' he asked looking them up and
down'..
'Yes' replied Eliza zombie.

'Any plants or vines on you?' replied Henry zombie as he put his hand on Eliza zombie's head and slowly spun her around.

And then did the same with Steve zombie, 'Good!'

'What-' began Steve zombie.

'Attention Please. Emergency. All personnel evacuate immediately. You have 3 minutes to reach Site Bravo'

'zombie Mum, zombie Dad' said Eliza zombie.

'We don't have enough time' said Henry zombie, 'Quick inside, everything will be ok' he ordered as he took Eliza zombie's and Steve zombie's hand and ran over the broken fence and into the main compound building.

Katie zombie burst in the front door screaming 'Eliza zombie, Steve zombie, Eliza zombie, Steve zombie'

Waiting by their zombie Car, David zombie let Andre zombie and Isabel zombie quickly scrabble inside.

'Love the spores'?

'What?' said David zombie and turned around to see Carolyn zombie walking towards him, 'Love the spores' repeated Carolyn zombie.

'Uhhh-'

Katie zombie ran out and punched Carolyn zombie squarely in the face.

'What-'

'If you weren't so busy staring at her chest you'd see the bloody -damn mushrooms and leaves growing out of her neck'.

'What?'

'I can't find Zah and Steve zombie' Smash! A black minibus had sped past their cave house and hit the car belonging to Mary and Percy zombie.

David and Katie zombie stared in wonder as (probably) Mary and Percy zombie stood in the now impassable road, shouting 'Love the spores' as the occupants of the minibus began escaping and ran down the hill/in to the playing field/across garden walls. Basically, anywhere except there.

'Attention Please. Emergency. All personnel to nearest de-com shelter. Purge in 2 minutes'.

David zombie looked back at the hill to see a yellow robed zombie standing in the middle of the road surrounded by a swirling mess of leaves, twigs and various parts of plants. A booming voice shouted 'I am the Zombie Toga King. You will love my spores'. David zombie watched in awe as the self-appointed Zombie Toga King looked up at the sky and exhaled a cloud of yellow dust. Beginning to stand near him were various villagers, David zombie thought he could make out Sebastian zombie, Julian zombie and even Chloë zombie all covered in vines and tendrils, especially around their heads. And bouncing around them were football size balls of wrapped vines. The Zombie Toga King finished exhaling and looked down at David zombie shouting 'All will hail the Zombie Toga King' and moving toward him.....

'Love my spores'?

David zombie shook his head, snapped out of his stupor and banged twice on the car roof, 'Everyone inside now' and all four ran into the house.

'Quick in the lift' said Henry zombie as he led Eliza and Ben zombie down a deserted corridor lit only by red flashing lights.

'What's going' on?' pleaded Eliza zombie.

'In the lift!' Demand a slightly panicking Henry zombie as he pulled them inside and hit the button saying Sub-level 7. And hit it again, and again, and again, 'C-mon!' and the doors finally shut and the lift began descending.
'Attention Please. Emergency. All personnel to nearest de-com shelter. Purge in 2 minutes.'
Eliza and Steve zombie both looked at Henry zombie wanting answers.
'I'll explain in a sec, we need to get in a de-com shelter' Isabel zombie slammed the front door and heard Carolyn zombie banging on it shouting 'love the spores'.
Katie zombie grabbed the CB, 'Eliza zombie, Steve zombie, where are you?
Eliza zombie, Steve zombie, answer me'.
Nothing.
'No!' shouted Katie zombie, holding the CB so tight that her nails were turning white.
Echoing across the village *'Attention Please.*
Emergency. All personnel to nearest de-com shelter.
Purge in 1 minute'.
More banging on the front door.
David zombie and Andre zombie dragged over a large bookcase to block the front door from being forced open.
'Upstairs in the bedroom' shouted David zombie.
'Yeah' agreed Andre zombie, 'away from the roots'.
'Eliza zombie, Steve zombie' repeated Katie zombie shouting in to the CB.
Nothing.
'Quick' said David zombie as he pulled Katie zombie upstairs following Andre zombie and Isabel zombie in to the bedroom.
'Attention Please. Emergency. All personnel to nearest de-com shelter. Purge in 60 seconds' echoed around the village.

Looking out of the widow they watched as the Zombie Toga King and his entourage slowly walked down the road, with vine entangled villagers (and perhaps Scare Farm zombie employees) either joining the procession or banging on doors and forcing their way in to caves. When David zombie suddenly noticed Elissa zombie waving madly out of an upstairs window at them. 'Perhaps they are with Elissa zombie?' hoped David zombie.

The lift reached Sub level 7 and a female voice kindly told them just that. *Sub Level 7 Mycology and Nutraceuticals.*

'Attention Please. Emergency. All personnel to nearest de-com shelter. Purge in 1 minute'.

Henry zombie jumped out first and briefly scanned the room, then focusing at a door with a green flashing light, 'In there' he pointed and ran over pulling Eliza zombie and Steve zombie with in. While he pushed them in, the door slammed shut followed by a series of locking sounds and a final long sucking sound as the room became air locked. 'Phew' said Henry zombie.

'Attention Please. Emergency. All personnel to nearest de-com shelter. Purge in 20 seconds'.

'Henry zombie' said Eliza zombie in a scared voice.

Henry zombie bent over Eliza zombie and Steve zombie in a protective manner as the announcement said *'Attention Please.*

Emergency. Purge in 10 seconds'

Eliza zombie squeezed Henry zombie's hand.

'Five, Four, Three, Two, One. Purge'

Printed in Great Britain
by Amazon